ROTHERHAM LIBRARY & INFORMATION SERVICE

KT-144-894

ClS

Illustrated by Cate Vaines

Chapter One

It was a warm summer morning. Pim yawned, stretched and wriggled out from under the wolfskins that made up her bed. Gramma was still snoring, but there was no sign of Pod and Little Nut.

"Where are they?" she wondered, and she ran to the doorway. "OUCH!" Pim rubbed her foot, and Gramma sat up with a jump. "What's happening?" she asked.

"Sorry, Gramma," Pim said. "I trod on something sharp." Gramma peered at the ground. "Nutshells. All over the floor. Clear them up, Pim." Pim shook her head. "It wasn't me, Gramma –"

"Doesn't matter." Gramma frowned at her.
Pim sighed and swooshed the shells into
a corner with a handful of straw. As soon
as she had finished she ran out into
the sunshine.

Pod and Little Nut were sitting under a tree watching Dada Boulder chipping at flints. They were both chewing, and Pim gave them a long, cold stare.

"You left nutshells all over the floor,"
she told them angrily.

Pod shrugged. "We were hungry."

"Hungry," repeated Little Nut. He flapped
his hand at a fly. "Go way!"

Pim picked up a leafy branch, and waved
it to and fro. Dada Boulder smiled at her.
"That's good. The flies are bad today."

Chapter Two

Dada Boulder worked fast. Bang, bang, bang he went with a heavy stone, and the flint began to look like a useful tool. Tap, tap, tap – it was sharp enough to use.

"Can I have a go?" Pod asked.

"Be careful," Dada Boulder warned.

"I know what to do," Pod said. He took the stone from Dada and banged it hard on a half-finished flint knife. The knife broke in two.

"I told you to be careful, Pod!" Dada sighed.

Pim leant forward. "Can I try?" she asked.

"Give me the branch, Pim! I'll scatter those flies!" Pod took the branch, but he waved it so wildly that he hit Dada Boulder on the head. Little Nut laughed, and Pod made a face. "Oops!"

"Pim," Dada said, "take your brothers away."

"But I haven't had a turn," Pim complained.

"And you need me to get rid of the flies." Pod waved the branch to and fro.

"I'd rather have flies than silly boys," Dada growled. "GO AWAY!"

Pim took Little Nut's hand. "Let's go down to the stream," she said. "Come on, Pod."

"Paddle?" asked Little Nut.

"Maybe," Pim told him.

Chapter Three

Mama Boulder was squatting by the stream,
a heap of wet clay beside her. She was
rolling it into long worms, and Little Nut
began to jump up and down.

"Little Nut play!"

"Me too," Pod said.

"This isn't play," Mama Boulder said.
"I'm making pots. Here!" She handed
a lump of clay to each of the children.
"See what you can do!"

Pod made his into a ball, threw it up in the air and caught it. "Look!" He threw it up again, but this time he missed and it landed on Little Nut.

Little Nut squealed happily, and threw his squishy lump at Pod. Pod threw it back, and moments later both of them were covered in slippy, slimy clay.

"POD! LITTLE NUT!" Mama Boulder was cross. "Stop it!"

"It's all right," Pod said. "It'll wash off in the stream," and he jumped in. Little Nut followed him, and they splooshed and splashed together.

Pim took no notice. She was carefully rolling her clay into long worms, just like Mama Boulder. "Is this right?" she asked.

"That's good," Mama Boulder said. "Very good. Shall I show you what to do next?"

But the next second – SPLOSH! Pod had chased Little Nut out of the stream, and Little Nut had tripped and fallen right on top of the rows of clay worms. Mama Boulder rose to her feet. "GO AWAY!" she roared.

Chapter Four

Pod and Little Nut looked at each other, then ran. Pim stayed where she was.

"Shall I help you make some more?" she asked, but Mama Boulder shook her head.

"Another time," she said. "Go and see what your brothers are doing."

Pim scowled, and went after Pod and Little Nut. "It's not fair," she thought. "They make a mess, and I have to clear it up. They get into trouble, and I have to look after them. I NEVER get to do what I want."

As Pim marched past Dada Boulder he called to her, but she didn't answer. She stomped into the hut and found Pod and Little Nut crawling round the floor.

"You're horrible, and I hate you!" she cried.

Pod looked surprised. "What did we do?"

"Do?" echoed Little Nut.

"You spoil everything!" Pim told them,

"and nobody EVER tells you off!"

"Yes they do," Pod said. "Gramma says we can't go out until EVERY SINGLE LITTLE BIT of nutshell is picked up and taken outside." Little Nut nodded. "Gramma cross."

Gramma grunted in agreement.

Pod came closer to Pim. "Dada is making you something special," he whispered. "REALLY?" Pim's eyes shone, and she hurried outside.

Chapter Five

Dada Boulder was under the tree. Pim came up and he looked at her. "Still angry?"

Pim giggled. "Not any more."

"Good," Dada Boulder said and held out something. "Here, this is for you."

Pim looked at the beautiful flint cutting
blade. "THANK YOU, Dada!"

"Now run down to the stream. Mama
is waiting for you. You can make a pot to
keep your knife safe." He winked at her.

"Safe from your brothers."

Pim stopped. Her brothers had been bad, but they would LOVE to make a pot. And it would be much more fun with three...

"If Pod and Little Nut promise to be good, can they come too?" she asked.

Dada Boulder stroked his chin while he thought. "Ask Gramma," he said at last.

Pim rushed back to the hut. "Can Pod and Little Nut come and make a pot with me? PLEASE? I'll help pick up nutshells!"

"It's up to them," Gramma grumbled. Pod and Little Nut stared at her, and then Little Nut grinned. "Little Nut is sorry."

"Me too," Pod agreed.

"Then you can all go," Gramma said.

Pim, Pod and Little Nut ran down to the stream. Mama and Dada Boulder were waiting for them. They got to work on making a beautiful pot ...

... and later on that day Gramma said that it was the best pot she had EVER seen! Perfect for keeping nuts in!

Life in the Stone Age

The Stone Age began around 2.6 million years ago. It was called the Stone Age as people used tools made of stone. They lived in huts made from animal skins and used special stones and dry grass to make fire. Stone Age people also learned to make clay pots for storing food and water. The pots were often decorated with patterns such as zig-zag lines.

Franklin Watts
First published in Great Britain in 2015
by The Watts Publishing Group

Series Editor: Melanie Palmer
Series Advisor: Catherine Glavina
Cover Designer: Cathryn Gilbert
Design Manager: Peter Scoulding

ISBN 978 1 4451 4265 4 (hbk)
ISBN 978 1 4451 4268 5 (pbk)
ISBN 978 1 4451 4267 8 (library ebook)

Printed in China

Franklin Watts
An imprint of
Hachette Children's Group
Part of The Watts Publishing Group
Carmelite House
50 Victoria Embankment
London EC4Y 0DZ

An Hachette UK Company
www.hachette.co.uk

www.franklinwatts.co.uk